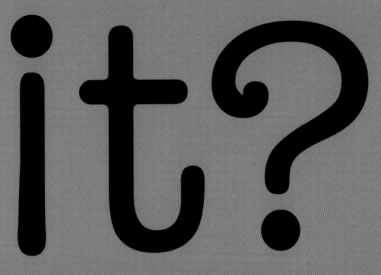

Etienne Delessert

Creative Editions

What is **it?**

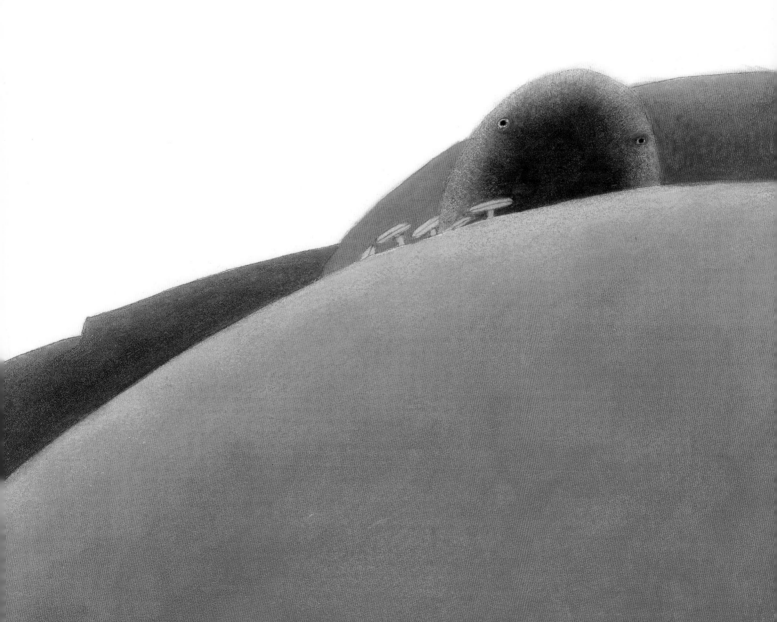

Is **it** a bumblebee? A dustball?

A cloud?

Where is **it** going?

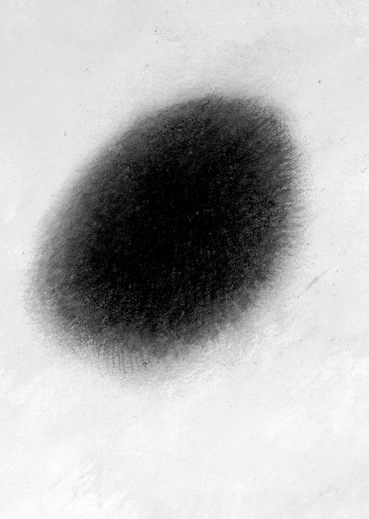

Follow **it**...

There **it** is!

Touch it!

it looks soft and fuzzy, but...

...is it a monster?

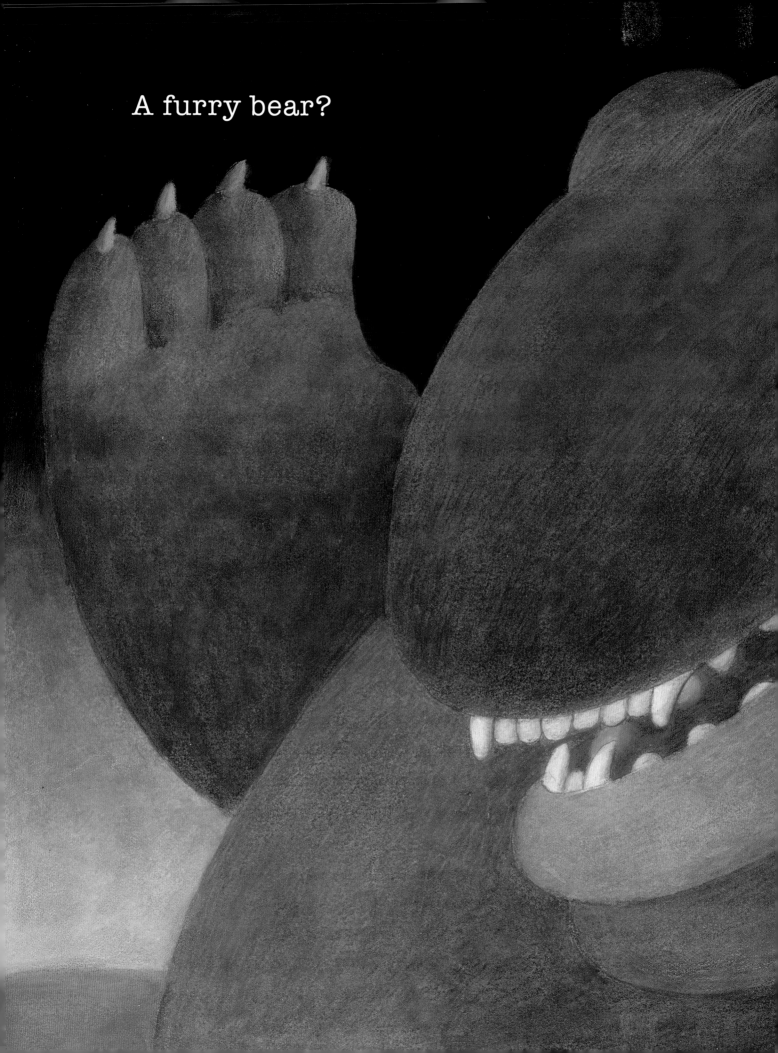

A furry bear?

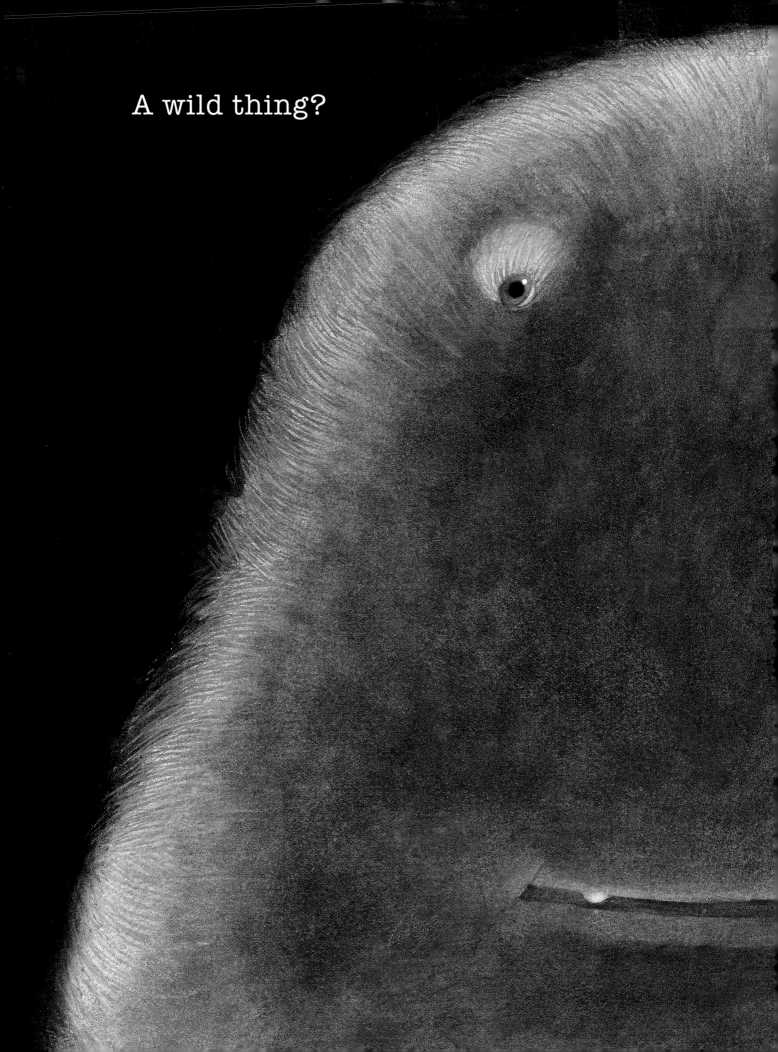

A wild thing?

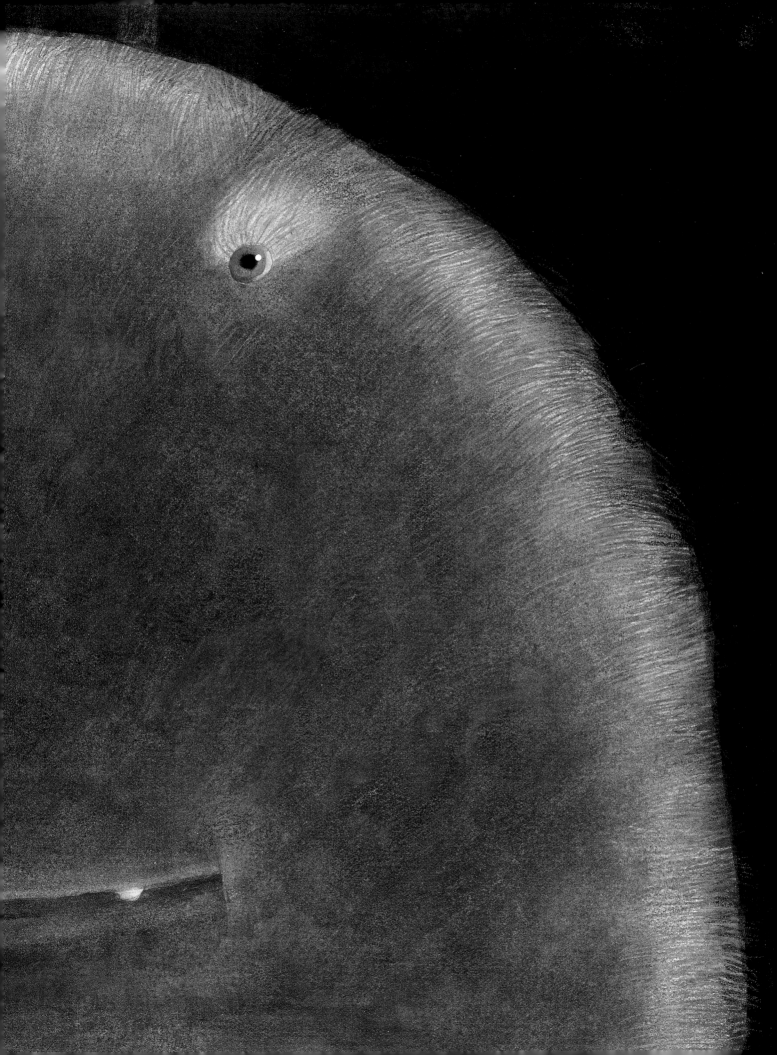

Let's give **it** some space!

Aw...Where'd **it** go?

Is **it** friend or foe?

Maybe **it** is a little thirsty?

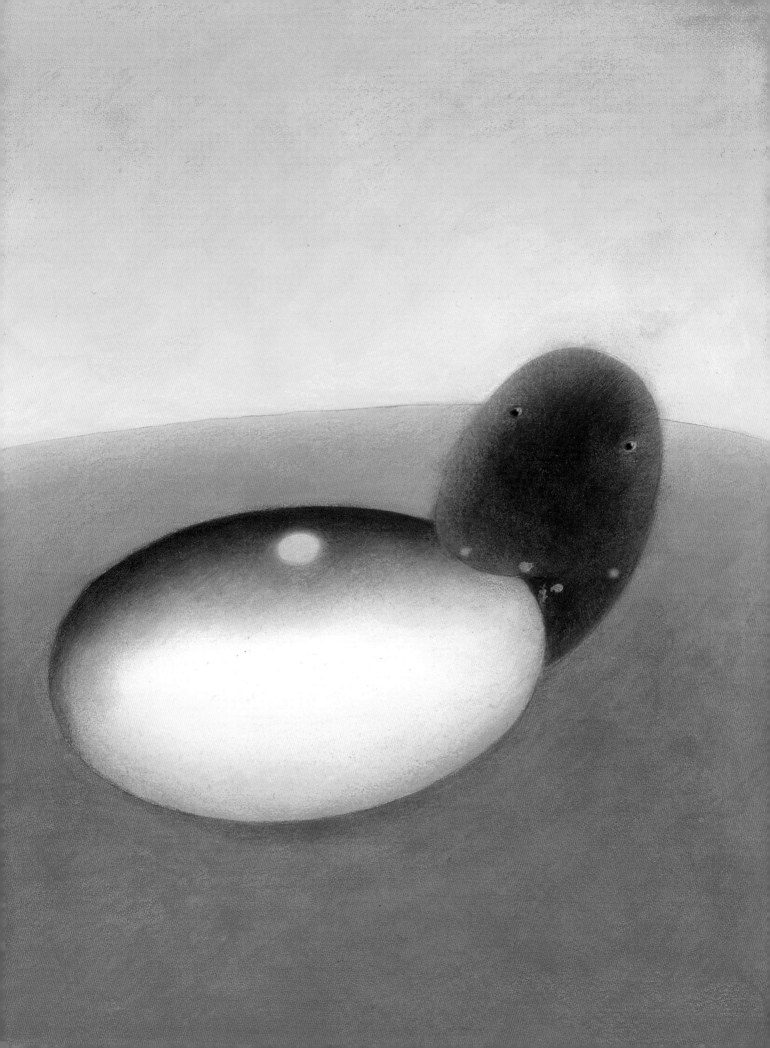

Hungry, too?

Look! **it** likes
breadcrumbs.

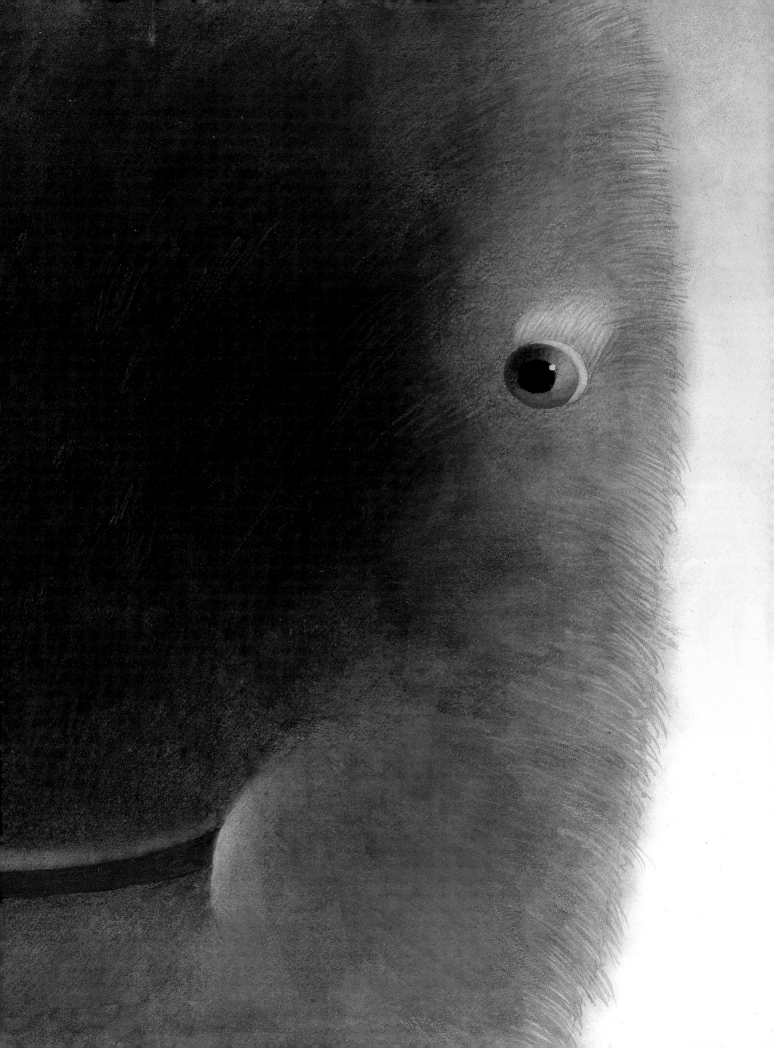

Does **it** want to play?

Slip **it** in your pocket.
It is your friend!

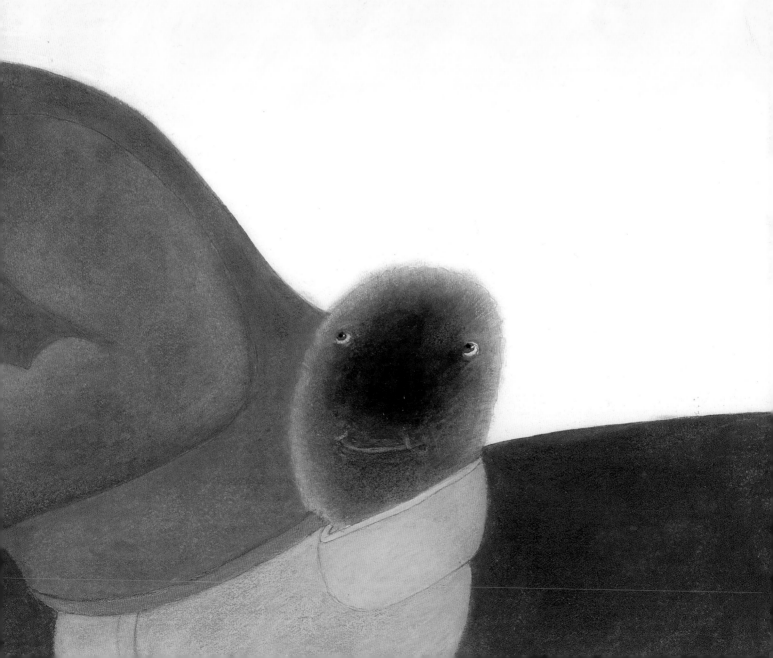

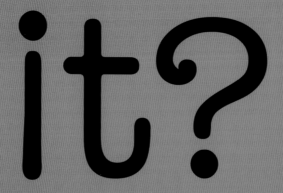

Text and illustrations copyright © 2019 by Etienne Delessert
Designed by Rita Marshall
Published in 2019 by Creative Editions
P.O. Box 227, Mankato, MN 56002 USA
Creative Editions is an imprint of The Creative Company
www.thecreativecompany.us

Library of Congress Cataloging-in-Publication Data
Names: Delessert, Etienne, author, illustrator.
Title: It? / by Etienne Delessert
Summary: In this modern fable of imaginative inquisition,
a boy finds and follows IT, wondering along the way if IT
is a monster, a furry bear, or perhaps a wild thing. In the
process, he makes a surprising new friend.
Identifiers: LCCN 2018054985 / ISBN 978-1-56846-345-2
Subjects: CYAC: Imagination—Fiction. / Friendship—Fiction.
Classification: LCC PZ7.D3832 It 2019   DDC [E]—dc23
First edition 9 8 7 6 5 4 3 2 1